There's an
OWL
in the Shower

Also by Jean Craighead George

The Moon of the Moles

The Moon of the Monarch Butterflies

The Moon of the Mountain Lions

The Moon of the Owls

The Moon of the Salamanders

The Moon of the Wild Pigs

The Moon of the Winter Bird

One Day in the Alpine Tundra

One Day in the Desert

One Day in the Prairie

One Day in the Tropical Rain Forest

One Day in the Woods

Shark Beneath the Reef

The Summer of the Falcon

The Talking Earth

Water Sky

Who Really Killed Cock Robin?
An Ecological Mystery

The Wounded Wolf

JEAN CRAIGHEAD GEORGE

Illustrated by Christine Herman Merrill

There's an
OWL
in the Shower

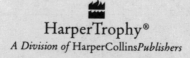

HarperTrophy®
A Division of HarperCollinsPublishers

There's an Owl in the Shower
Text copyright © 1995 by Julie Productions, Inc.
Illustrations copyright © 1995 by Christine Herman Merrill
All rights reserved. No part of this book may be used or reproduced in any manner
whatsoever without written permission except in the case of brief quotations embodied
in critical articles and reviews. Printed in the United States of America.
For information address HarperCollins Children's Books,
a division of HarperCollins Publishers, 10 East 53rd Street, New York, NY 10022.

Library of Congress Cataloging-in-Publication Data
George, Jean Craighead, date
    There's an owl in the shower / by Jean Craighead George ; illustrated by Christine
Herman Merrill.
        p.   cm.
    Summary: Because protecting spotted owls has cost Borden's father his job as a logger
in the old growth forest of northern California, Borden intends to kill any spotted owl
he sees, until he and his father find themselves taking care of a young owlet.
    ISBN 0-06-024891-2. — ISBN 0-06-024892-0 (lib. bdg.)
    ISBN 0-06-440682-2 (pbk.)
    [1. Spotted owls—Fiction.   2. Logging—Fiction.   3. Endangered species—Fiction.
4. Logging—Fiction.   5. Parent and child—Fiction.]
I. Merrill, Christine Herman, ill.   II. Title.
PZ7.G2933Th   1995   94-38893
[Fic]—dc20   CIP
                                                                                   AC

Typography by Al Cetta
❖
First Harper Trophy edition, 1997

To the members of
the Willow Creek Northern Spotted Owl Study—
Rocky, Alan, Chris, and Peter

Contents

1

A Good Owl

Borden Watson braked his bike and jumped off. He wheeled it across the narrow logging road and into the dark forest. Leaning it against a tree, he took his rifle from its carrier and put a bullet in the chamber.

A cool green silence wrapped around him. He breathed deeply, then stepped onto the needle-carpeted ground and walked a soundless distance. Ankle deep in ferns and wildflowers, he stopped in a grove of trees. The trees were so enormous that one alone, standing in the middle of a logging road, could block trucks in two directions.

Borden was in the old-growth forest of the Pacific Coast in northern California, a land blessed with abundant rain and sun, a temperate climate, and deep soils.

He did not see this wild wealth. He was in the old-growth forest for one purpose: to shoot owls—spotted owls.

He hated them.

His eyes cruised up the trunk of an enormous Douglas fir. They peered past the large low branches, up past a floral burst of limbs where a pine siskin cheeped, and on up to a cluster of needles two hundred feet above the forest floor. Just below the needle spray was a large nest of sticks. He grinned.

"You," he said aloud. "You owl, in that nest. You're dead, the minute you stick your head up."

It was almost twilight, and the owl, Borden reasoned, should be awake and ready to go out hunting. He thought about his father and cried out, "My dad doesn't have a job because of you. He can't cut any more big trees because of you."

Shouting seemed to help the pain Borden

had felt since his father had lost his job with the lumber company. His father had told him that a judge had stopped all sale of the trees on public lands in the Northwest until the United States Forest Service could come up with a plan to save the spotted owl. It lived in the old-growth forests, and the forests were being cut down for lumber. The gentle owl was on the brink of extinction.

The government, it seemed to Borden, liked owls better than people.

Borden thought about this and grew angrier. "He's the best tree cutter from here north through Canada to Alaska," he shouted to the bird in the nest hole.

"He can put a giant tree right down on the earth without hitting a single tree around it. He can do that." He lifted his rifle. He had more to say.

"He's the best of the cutters, and the cutters are the most important people in the whole lumber business. And their work is very, very dangerous. Limbs and trees can fall and kill or injure them. They have to be smart people." He paused, then went on.

"My pop is famous. He won the National Tree Cutters' Award—" He smiled pridefully, then remembered. "But because of you, he can't work."

Borden caught his breath and thought about what he had just said. He did not understand why a little owl could stop honest, hardworking men like his father from cutting down trees, but it had happened. Now his father was out of work, and it was painful for the whole Watson family.

His mother had been forced to take a job in the school cafeteria. Borden had mowed lawns to help, but that was in the summer. Through the winter and into late spring he, too, was out of work.

Sally, his older sister, with her pale-blue eyes and bush of red stringy curls, was also upset. She had stopped playing soccer with her friends, and every day except Tuesdays came home right after school. She would go to her room and close the door. She wouldn't talk about spotted owls when Borden and his father ranted against them.

Borden suspected she was embarrassed that Pop didn't have a job. She didn't need to be. She could be angry, maybe, but not embarrassed. Many fathers were out of work in the lumber town of Fresta. Stores had closed, and businesses and lumber companies had failed. Almost everyone was suffering, but that did not seem to matter to Sally. She went on soothing her hurt behind her closed door. Borden did not criticize her. He understood why she felt as she did. Their father was Leon Watson, big, noisy, protective. They thought nothing could happen to him. But it had, and that was very upsetting. A hero had been felled by a measly little bird.

All spring, Borden thought up plans to get his father's job back. None were any good. He just didn't understand why an owl could stop a man like his pop from cutting down trees.

When Judge Kramer came down the street

on his way to the post office one school morning, Borden caught up to him and put the question to him.

"There's a law," said the impeccably dressed judge, adjusting his tie. "It's called the Endangered Species Act. It states that no one can destroy threatened and endangered creatures or the habitats they live in. If they do, they will be fined, put in jail, or both." He looked at Borden.

"Our northern spotted owl is a threatened species. He can only live in old-growth forests and nest in big tall trees. When we cut them down, he dies."

Borden thought about that. Judge Kramer continued. "The problem is this: The agencies that take care of our public lands—the U.S. Forest Service and the Bureau of Land Management—violated the nation's environmental laws. They permitted lumber companies to cut recklessly and too fast. The owls are being wiped off the face of the earth. Mountainsides are eroding. A judge in Seattle ordered all timber sales, and therefore cutting, to stop until there is a workable plan to save the owl."

"We're going to save the owl, not the people?" Borden asked.

"The owl is telling the people we aren't managing our forests right. Save the owl, and you save the people, too. We need forests." His heel tapped the sidewalk like the tick of a clock. "In some places in Washington state, only six pairs of spotted owls remain on six million acres of old growth that were cut in the past. That's trouble for the owls, and trouble for us."

"Can't the owls move?"

"They can't. When the big trees are gone, the owls will die."

"But Pop's company leaves some big trees for the owls."

"Too far apart. The owls can't hear each other, and if they can't hear each other, they can't find each other. If they can't find each other, they can't mate; and if they can't mate—no more owls."

Borden frowned.

"It's a terrible thing no matter how you look at it," Judge Kramer said. "Cut the trees, and the owls become extinct. Stop felling them, and the cutters—"

"—become extinct," said Borden. "And that's terrible."

For the next week, Borden put his mind once more to solving the problem of owls, trees, and cutters. To think more clearly, he rode his bike out to the Trinity River after school and climbed up on his favorite rock. He decided the lumber companies should cut the trees anyway. Once trees were down, no one could put them back up, so the mills might as well sell them. Then he remembered that Judge Kramer had said anyone who destroyed the homeland of a threatened species would be fined or put in jail, and he thought again.

The next day he was biking through the little flower-filled park in the middle of town when he braked to a stop. A spotted owl hung by its neck from a lamppost.

"Now, there's a good owl," he said.

Borden saw what must be done. It was that simple. He headed out for the mountains.

2
Enrique

Borden leaned against a young fir tree and recalled the owl hanging from the lamppost. It had bright white spots and walnut-brown feathers. Easy to identify. He smiled. He was a good shot.

A woodpecker drilled to his left. He listened to the rapid hammering. Overhead a small flock of golden-crowned kinglets sang a series of thin, wiry notes, then chattered softly. Borden thought their voices sounded more like the wind brushing the needles than birdsong. He wanted to look at them but dared not. He must keep his eyes on the nest.

"Owl," he said aloud. "Come on out. I know you're in there. My pop showed me your home last year. He said the cutters call you Enrique. You took my pop's job. Well I'm going to fix that."

He could not say more. The words coming out were crinkled with emotion.

A black-tailed deer got to her feet in a grove of ferns. She saw Borden and stood tree-still. Gingerly she sniffed the air, then caught the scent of him and bolted. Borden turned in time to see her vanish into a swatch of rhodo-dendrons. Borden looked back at the nest and fingered the trigger on his gun.

Some distance away in a Douglas fir at the edge of the logging road, an owl awoke. He was red-brown from head to toe, chunky, and about a foot and a half tall. He looked more like a redwood stump than an owl. The owl shook, and a cloud of dust from the logging road puffed out from him. He shook again. Another cloud appeared, then one more. When the dust was gone, there sat a beautiful spotted owl.

He was reminiscent of the stars in a midnight sky. Two black holes were his eyes.

Around his face, dark feathers formed a heart-shaped disc that swept sound to his ears. White eyebrows reflected light into his eyes. He was Enrique, devoted father, great hunter, and one of a few remaining northern spotted owls.

He turned his head slowly from side to side, not so much to see, but to listen. Then he ran his beak down the rachis, or hollow barrel, of a wing feather. He pulled it far back and let go. It snapped into place noiselessly. Soft edges along this and all his flight feathers muted their sound. He flew in silence.

Enrique swung his head back and forth, then up and down, as he listened to the music of the forest. One ear was lower than the other, giving him "sound vision" sharper than an eagle's eyes. He heard crickets and twittering birds, and finally, by turning his head, he heard his highway through the tree limbs. Spreading his wings, Enrique soared off, maneuvering among the twigs and branches by sound.

Borden heard nothing as Enrique passed

overhead and alighted on a limb above the nest.

"Who Who Who Who ooooo," the bird called to his mate. She was brooding their two owlets in the deep center of the stick nest that had been built years ago by a hawk and taken over by Enrique and his mate of many years.

Borden clicked off the safety on his rifle.

That small sound reached Enrique. The spotted owl is required to have ears that are eyes. Enrique lived high in the forest canopy and hunted for creatures who romped in the fog and mist more than a hundred feet below. He "saw" Borden through that click, then brought him into focus with his eyes and sat still.

Borden circled the tree, peering into the high limbs. After a brief search, he saw the roundish owl shape. Quickly he aimed, holding his breath so he would not jerk when he pulled the trigger. Then for some reason he hesitated, and in that instant the owl faded from sight. It was too dark.

"Nuts," he said.

He climbed slowly up the steep ravine in the darkness and found his bike. Wheeling it out onto the road, he turned and looked into the gray-black owl grove.

"I'll be back," he said. He wheeled off down the mountain road toward his home in

the lumber town of Fresta on the Trinity River. The town was thirty miles inland from the Pacific Ocean in the Trinity National Forest.

Enrique listened until Borden rounded the bend and sped away. The gunman gone, he concentrated on finding food. He rotated his head almost all the way over his back. His ears were tapping into the sound waves from flying squirrels, deer mice, and wood rats.

Enrique could also hear the gap in the

forest where a group of ancient Douglas firs and incense cedars had been cut down by Borden's father and his crew. The empty space whistled and whined. From a distance came a vaster sound. It was created by the treeless north side of the mountain. The cutters had clear-cut here, sawing down every tree, big and small, until the mountainside was bare. With them went Enrique's hunting perches and food supply. He was forced to search farther from home.

He was wide awake now. He floated down to the limb beside his nest and called softly. Two owlets thrust their heads out from under their mother's wings and screamed. Their raspy hunger calls drove Enrique onto his wings, and he flew off to hunt for them.

Enrique had to feed not only the owlets, but also his mate. She could not leave their young. They had recently hatched and were scantily feathered. At the top of the giant trees, the air was either too cold or too hot for the owlets. The female stayed with them for at least two weeks after their hatching, to brood and regulate their temperatures.

Enrique alighted on the branch of an ancient Douglas fir four miles away. It stood in several hundred acres of old-growth forest, part of his five square miles of home range. The flying squirrels were plentiful here. Enrique lifted the feathers over his ears and let in the sounds.

He heard barred owl nestlings snapping their beaks in a hollow in the tree where he sat. Then like a sword-edged wind, the mother barred owl rocketed down upon him. Talons spread, she boomed her tiger call. Barred owls look very much like spotted owls with their solid black eyes and pale horizontal markings, and are often confused with them. They are more aggressive than spotted owls, however, and take over their trees and home range. Chain saws and barred owls were making Enrique's task of providing food for his family very difficult.

Enrique took off. He soared over a clear-cut

mountainside to another old-growth forest, where he caught a flying squirrel. He carried it back to his mate to share with the owlets. He returned the long distance and hunted until dawn. He caught only one more squirrel. The owlets were still calling for food when daylight sent him back to his roost above the logging road.

At sunrise, the huge logging trucks rolled up the mountain and passed through the public lands where Enrique lived. They were on their way to the privately owned forests of the logging companies. These forests were managed by their owners to produce crops of trees in the same way farmers raise wheat and corn. The trees were cut and seedlings planted. Some seventy-five years in the future, they would be harvested. The logging ban did not apply to the private forests.

The trucks passed below Enrique, stirring up the dust, and by noon he looked like a redwood stump again.

3
Problems

Borden did not return to the owl nest as soon as he thought he would. Jimmy Olden, his best friend, got him a job after school at Mike's Gas Station.

Mike's had become the town's west-side meeting place after the government ban. Here owl lovers ran into owl haters. They argued, shouted, and shook fists at one another. Both sides were convinced they were right. Borden listened, but he was perfectly clear about where he stood. He polished bumper stickers that said **I LIKE SPOTTED OWLS FRIED**. He left the dirt on the ones that read **SAVE THE SPOTTED OWL**.

One day his father, Leon Watson, pulled up at the gas station. He stepped out of his truck just as Paul James, the leader of the owl lovers, stepped out of his car.

"Good morning, Mr. Watson," Paul James said.

"Humph," Leon growled. "When are you going to care more about people than owls?"

Paul James had heard this so many times, he was tired of it.

"The trouble is, you loggers don't see the problem," he said, his voice edgy. "The decline of the spotted owl is like a canary in a coal mine. We are being warned that the environment is not safe."

"My environment is sure not safe," Leon snapped. His shirt sleeves were rolled up, and the muscles in his arms looked as if they were about to go into action. Paul James, a science teacher at the high school as well as an environmentalist, turned his attention to filling his gas tank.

"The spottys," he said, "are telling us we have not properly managed our forests."

"You're crazy," Leon snapped, coming

toward him. "The owls aren't telling us anything. For years the Forest Service and the Bureau of Land Management have been telling us to cut the old growth. They ought to know what's good for us."

"Well, they don't seem to," said Paul James. He turned and faced Leon. "They were warned years ago that the spotty was in trouble. Environmentalists told them they should change their policy. They didn't. The spottys kept declining until they now are a threatened species. When the environment—the water, fish, and soil—began to deteriorate, the law kicked in. You guys are suffering for other people's mistakes."

"Owls be damned," Leon snapped. He turned off the pump and headed for the office to pay. "My kids are hungry," he said as he passed Paul James. "In my book, kids come first." He reached out and tapped the teacher on the chest.

Taken by surprise, Paul James swung out his arm and caught Leon across the chin. Leon grabbed Paul's arm and wrestled him to the ground. Borden, knowing how strong his father was, ran to the telephone and dialed 911.

At that moment, two more loggers arrived in a pickup.

"Knock him out," one of them shouted. Paul James wrestled free of Leon's grip and got to his feet. He stepped back.

Leon strode to within inches of him. His bronze-colored hair was wet with perspiration; his brown eyes glittered under shaggy brows. Borden saw his fists clench.

"Pop, don't," he yelled, and stepped between them. One of the newcomers grabbed Borden by the back of his shirt and yanked him away. A stranger walking by thought he saw the big logger picking on a boy, pushed him back, and told him to lay off. The man turned and socked the stranger.

A student who was filling his tank saw Leon drive a powerful blow into Paul James's stomach. The student jumped on Leon and held his arms. Leon laughed, expanded his chest, and bent forward. The student was catapulted through the air. He landed on the grass with a thud just as the police drove up. Borden ran to help him.

Two officers stepped out of the patrol car.

Leon took another poke at Paul James. Paul James returned it. An officer grabbed him. The other took Leon by the arm and pulled him back. The fighting stopped.

"Hey, I'm sorry," Paul James said to Leon.

Borden looked at his father. He hoped his dad would apologize. He did not. He shook his fist at Paul James.

"Careful, Leon," Captain Ryan said. "I don't want to have to arrest you for disorderly conduct."

"I'm not disorderly," Leon said. "Society is."

On his way to the office to pay for his gas, Leon gave Borden a friendly poke in the ribs.

"Arrest that man," the stranger shouted and pointed to Leon. "If you don't, I will. I'll make a citizen's arrest." The two officers looked at each other helplessly. Fights and short tempers were common in Fresta since the ban, but no crimes had been committed. This spat was over. Both men were calm. The policemen did not want to arrest Leon

Watson or Paul James. The stranger sensed this.

"I'm coming with you to the precinct and see that you arrest them. If you don't, I will. We can't put up with fights and brawls every day."

"All right, all right," said Sergeant Ryan. "I'll do it. I'll deliver a warrant for his arrest tonight. He's not going anywhere."

"What about him?" said one of the loggers, pointing to Paul James. "He started it."

"Him, too," said Captain Ryan. He got into his patrol car and slammed the door. The policemen drove off. The stranger followed.

"Tough times," Mike said when Leon paid for his gas. He shook his head. "It's really terrible not to have a job."

Leon nodded and strode to his truck. He slammed the door. Paul James had paid for his gas and driven off. Leon followed.

Borden watched his pop turn right on the main street and head toward home. He was upset. His father was going to be arrested. It was not fair.

He thought of the owl on the mountain and knew it was time to carry out his plan.

4
The Owlets

Two weeks had passed since Enrique had been hunted by Borden. They had been stressful weeks for the owl and his family. Food was difficult to find. He could not hunt the fir forest where the barred owl lived, or the north slope of the mountain that had been clear-cut. He had to fly to more and more distant areas of his home range, and he caught less and less prey for his efforts. He hunted from sunset to dawn.

The shortage of food unsettled Enrique's mate. The owlets were growing weak, yet they were not feathered well enough for her to leave them and help Enrique hunt. As each night passed, they all grew more hungry. The owlets constantly begged with opened mouths, a sight and sound that aroused her instincts to feed. She shifted restlessly.

One night Enrique caught nothing. The hunger cries of the owlets drove the female to the limb beside the nest. She listened. A black-tailed deer cropped leaves below; a pine marten ran along tree limbs; but she heard no flying-squirrel feet. She spread her wings and flew to a distant valley of old trees. The forest did not belong to her and Enrique, but to her own parents. She had lived there for the first six months of her life and knew the forest well.

She alighted on a family hunting post, a broken limb above a tan-oak grove. Abruptly, she flattened her feathers to her body in fear. She was not at ease on her parents' property. They had driven her off when she was mature. Territory belongs to adult pairs. The young must go. She listened, expecting them to attack her again, but heard only the wind bringing fog in from the Pacific Ocean. She flew deeper into the property. Near the top of a giant

Douglas fir, she alighted and tuned in to the night sounds. At first she heard nothing, then in the foggy distance she recognized the boom of her father's voice. He was calling to his mate. She waited. No mate answered him. He called insistently, over and over again. He was asking a female to come take the place of the mate he had lost. No one answered. He went on calling.

A chipmunk came out of its hole in an oxalis garden. It rustled leaves on its way to a gooseberry plant. Enrique's mate heard it. She crouched to drop down on it when a splash of rain jammed her hearing. She bobbed her head up and down. She twisted from front to back, trying to catch the sound of the chipmunk again. She could not. The rain was too noisy. But she did hear a coyote call from the grasslands near the top of the mountain and remembered the chipmunks there.

Eager to leave her parents' property, she flew swiftly over the tops of the great trees to an ancient oak forest that grew higher up the mountain than the Douglas firs. She alighted on a leafy limb.

A Steller's jay, sleeping on a perch below her, rustled its feathers to flip off the rain. The owl heard, and struck. Using her wings like oars, she maneuvered the bird between the limbs to the ground. Taking a firm grip with her feet, she pushed off and carried the jay back to her young. One bird was all she got that night.

The next night when Enrique and his mate had gone hunting, the hungry owlets climbed out of the deep nest, using their beaks and claws. Sitting on the rim side by side, they listened to the small music of the midnight treetops. They could hear the pine siskins and kinglets shifting their feet in their shelters in the dark. The owlets turned their heads until their ears told them exactly where the little birds were. Then rain splattered onto the fir needles, and the owlets heard only taps and splatters. When the air grew cold, they huddled together and watched for their parents.

It rained for a week. This was unusual. Mid-May is the beginning of the dry season in the northwest coastal forest. Over the eons, spotted owls have adapted to this season by timing the arrival of their young with the good weather. This year, nature was failing the spotted owls on the mountain.

Despite the rain, Enrique traveled each

night over his home range hunting for food. He came upon the oak forest and caught a young jay that was sleeping alone.

He carried it to the owlets. His mate was not there to feed them. Their cries provoked him to tear the prey into small pieces and put them into the gaping mouths. While he fed them, the young male gazed into his face. The owlet saw the disc of dark feathers, the vibrissae that stood out like a sunburst around Enrique's beak, and the dark soulful eyes. The owlet looked and looked until the face was printed on his memory.

The next day the rain fell in torrents. It ran down tree trunks, bounced off limbs, then soaked into the deep soil of the owl grove. Beyond the owls' nest on the treeless mountainside, it hit the ground with the force of bullets, dug up the soil, and carried it down to Fire Creek. The muddy run off clogged the gills of the young salmon, and in the creek hundreds died.

The rain stopped in the late afternoon,

and the mother owl went out to hunt. The owlets huddled in a spot of warm sunshine. Suddenly, a powerful wind roared off the ocean. It sped through the space where Borden's father had felled the big Douglas firs. With no trees to check its force, it hit the owls' tree with hurricane strength.

The owlets were swept from the nest. The little male grabbed at tree limbs, fell, spread his stubby wings, and was blown toward the logging road. He crashed onto the forest floor. The female, who is always larger than the male, landed not far from him. Hunched and frightened, the two owlets sat on their heels staring at the rain-spangled flowers into which they had fallen.

5

Kidnapped

The owlets were out of the nest too soon. Under normal conditions, they would have fluttered to the ground in mid-June and taken short flights to low limbs. There they would have sat while their parents fed them for another month, or until they could fly and hunt on their own. Their growth and skills were carefully timed to fit into the forest life. These young were off schedule. They were not even old enough to have developed the instinct to get off the ground. They just sat in the rain, wide-eyed and hungry.

The big female owlet saw a dry shelter under an enormous log and hopped toward it. A pine marten saw her and leaped down from a limb. Owlet feathers burst into the air as the pine marten killed her.

The male owlet wiggled under the arbutus leaves and sat still. Before daylight, he shook the rain from his wings, making just enough noise for his mother to locate him. She flew to the ground with a morsel of food in her beak. He reached for it, but she did not feed him. She hopped a few steps and dangled the food again. The owlet followed her until she lured him out of the flowers to the base of a rhododendron bush. She climbed up it, and dangled the morsel. He climbed after her, using beak and claws. The mother owl moved higher. The owlet climbed higher. When she was under a cluster of big leaves on a low limb, she waited for him to join her, then fed him.

The owlet closed his eyelids with their lashes of tiny exquisite feathers. He was asleep as a fog rolled in and dampened the mosses and ferns.

About four hours later, he heard his father's

resounding voice through the vanishing fog. The owlet spread his stubby wings and flew. They could not keep him airborne, and he came down to earth in the arbutus garden.

Head up, listening for his father, his eyes adapting to the light, he suddenly felt the ground shake. Turning his head, he looked up at Borden.

"Hi," the startled boy said. "What are you doing here?"

The owlet blinked and snapped his beak to warn the animal before him that he was a predator and an owl.

"You all alone?" Borden asked, searching the trees for his parents. He knelt down and examined the fluffy white owlet before him.

"You haven't got any spots," he said. "That's good. If you did, I would have to shoot you."

The owlet sat and stared at Borden.

"Aren't you afraid?" Borden asked, charmed by the owlet's bravery. He stroked the wet head. The bird looked at him fear-lessly. Borden picked him up.

"Now what do I do with you?" he asked,
and felt the breastbone of the little bird press
against his hand. "Boy, are you skinny."

The owlet turned his head upside down,
the better to see Borden. Borden grinned.
The owlet looked more like an elf than a bird.
He suddenly wanted to take the little elf

home. He examined the downy breast feathers carefully.

"You're a barred owl," he said. "Barred owls don't have spots. They also have solid black eyes like yours. I'm going to call you Bardy, the barred owl."

Gently tucking the owlet in his shirt, he found his bike and left the forest. Bardy, feeling the warmth of Borden's body, snuggled against him and rested.

Together they went down the mountain.

6

Bardy

"What is *that?*" bellowed Leon Watson.

"An owlet," Borden said, easing Bardy onto the kitchen table. "He fell out of his nest." The bird, now dry and fluffy, looked up at Leon, his huge mysterious eyes seeking the father's dark eyes in a bearded face.

"Shoot him," Leon said.

"He hasn't got any spots, does he?"

"No."

"So he's not a spotty. He's a barred owl."

"So what? Shoot him anyway." Leon was still in his pajamas, although it was nearly dinnertime. Ever since he had been out of work, he had let himself go. His hair was stringy and in need of shampooing. His beard was untrimmed. He looked like an unmade bed, but he didn't care.

"What are you going to do with him?" he growled.

"Feed him until he can fly, then take him back to the mountain and let him go."

"Shoot him."

"No," said Borden. "He's not a spotted owl. I only shoot spotted owls." He stood silently looking at the fearless little owlet with the large soulful eyes. "I think," he said slowly, "that we should raise him and show the owl lovers that we don't hate all owls—just spotted owls."

"But we do," roared Leon, the veins in his thick neck swelling as he spoke. "Shoot him!" He was not in a good mood. Last night Captain Ryan had come to the house in extreme embarrassment and handed him a warrant for his arrest.

"Am I going to jail?" Leon had asked, aghast.

"No," the officer had said. "I have to give

you this. You can either come before the judge and tell him your story and hope he lowers the fine, or pay the fifty dollars and be done with it."

"Fifty dollars!" Leon had boomed. "I'll talk to the judge." The elfin owlet sitting on the table was a reminder of all his troubles, and Leon's ire was aroused.

"Shoot him," he repeated.

"No, I only shoot spotted owls," Borden said again. "This is not a spotted owl. Besides, he likes me." The bird shook his feathers, and bits of down floated into the air. He bobbed his round head up, then down, and fluttered his stubby wings, all the while looking up at Leon.

"What's the matter with him?" Leon asked.

"He's hungry," said Borden.

"What're you going to feed him?"

"Chicken, I guess. He's a meat eater."

"Chicken!" roared Leon. "That's too expensive. Feed him mice."

"I don't have time to catch mice."

"What do you mean, you don't have time? Set mousetraps in the riverside field up at the abandoned Russell farm, and *snap*, you've got forty of 'em."

"I can't go running back and forth to the riverside field," Borden said. "I have to go to school and work at the gas station."

"Well, you're not going to feed him chicken."

"Hamburger?"

"No." The downy owlet, who had been standing on his feet all this time, sunk weakly to his heels. He fluttered his wings and opened his mouth. He called to Leon. The big cutter looked at him.

"All that wing-beating is some kind of bird talk," he said, distracted at last from the previous night's nightmare. "I think he's asking me to feed him. Looks like a kid begging." Borden saw the beginning of a smile on Pop's lips. It crinkled the corners of his eyes.

"Can I keep him?" he asked. "Can I, Pop?

He's neat. I'll let him go when he can fly."
The owlet blinked.

"You know, Borden," Leon said, thinking
aloud. "Might not be a bad idea to be kind to a
barred owl." He studied the little bird, who was
still staring at him. "I'll tell you what. I'll catch
mice for him if you don't have the time. Maybe
the judge will let me off when he hears I've
helped save a poor little owlet. You can't be all

bad if you save a bird." He sat down and put his elbows on the table and his chin in his fists.

"How about it?" he said, looking at the owlet. "What did you call him, Borden?"

"Bardy."

"How about it, Bardy? Want me for a mom?" He chuckled. "I'll tell the judge how we saved your life." He pushed back from the table and threw his shoulders back, chest out. "Then, when he lets me off, I'll wring your neck." He laughed heartily and put his elbows back down on the table.

The owlet saw the cave Leon had made with his arms and body and ran into it. It was the nearest thing he could find to a shelter in this new cold and angular world. Feeling secure, he bent his knees and sat down on his heels and insteps. He closed his tired eyes.

Leon sat up, removing the shelter. The owlet got to his feet. Leon leaned over him again, and the owlet sat down.

"Seems he wants a shelter," Leon said. "There's a wooden box in the garage by the

920 Jonserred super chain saw. Go get it, and we'll fix it up for him."

When Bardy was in the box with newspapers spread, Leon put him beside the kitchen stove. He placed a piece of plywood over the box to make it dark and cozy. Then he went to the garage for mousetraps.

"Come on, Borden," he said. "We've got a few hours before dark. Let's catch some mice. This little fellow is going to die if we don't feed him—and I want to keep him until I go to court."

They hiked several miles to the riverside field. It was famous for its numerous voles and mice. Paul James took his science classes there to study not only the little rodents but the birds of prey that came to eat them. As Leon and Borden approached, two red-tailed hawks and one black-shouldered kite were circling above this predator supermarket. A northern harrier hawk sat on the fencepost. Behind him the river gleamed red in the sunset.

Borden had been there with Sally when

she was taking Paul James's class, so he was able to show his father what a mouse highway was. He pointed to a groove in the grass and told Leon to set a trap there. They put out ten traps on the grass highway, then went back to the fence and sat down. Borden opened a soda can, took a sip, and passed it to Leon. He brushed it aside.

"I can't get over that Paul James hitting me in the face," he said. "Did he think I was going to take that? What does he expect a man to do? Smile and turn the other cheek? Not me."

"Aw, Pop, forget it," Borden said. "Pretty soon there won't be any spotted owls, and you can log again."

"How do you know?"

"Judge Kramer told me so. He said they need big trees, lots of them."

"But we left lots of big trees for them, just like the government told us to do."

"Judge Kramer said they're too far apart. He said the owls can't hear each other, and if they can't hear each other, they can't find each other, and if they can't find each other, they can't mate, and if they can't mate—no more owls. So all we have to do is wait."

"That irks me," said Leon. "We were told we were leaving plenty of big trees for the owls." He fell silent, leaned against the fence-post, and watched the swallows dip gracefully over the river.

An hour later, they had two mice.

7
A Mouse-Tail Message

Upon arriving home from the riverside field, Borden pushed back the plywood cover on the owl box and peered in. He sighed with relief. Bardy was still alive. Leon leaned over his shoulder. The owlet saw him, fluttered his wings, and called hungrily. Borden dropped a mouse at his feet.

"That ought to hush him up," he said. It did not, so Leon dropped the other one.

They waited, but Bardy did not eat. He just looked at the mice, then up at Leon. His black eyes concentrated on Leon's. He cried for food.

"Why isn't he eating?" Borden asked.

"Put the cover on," said Leon. "Owls eat in the dark." Borden did. The phone rang. It

was Jimmy Olden asking him to work for him at the gas station for a few hours. His mother wanted him to baby-sit.

"Sure," Borden answered, and hung up. "Tell Mom I'll be home late," he said, putting on his slicker as he ran out the door. "I'm working for Jimmy."

That night around midnight Leon awoke. He put on his bathrobe and went quietly into the kitchen. He lifted the plywood cover. Bardy stared up at him.

"Still alive," he said sternly. "Good." The two mice lay untouched at his feet.

"Why don't you eat?" he asked. "You can't die on me, you know." He picked up a mouse and dangled it, tail down, before Bardy. Bardy looked at Leon, fluttered his wings, and begged.

"What're you trying to tell me?" Leon asked, kneeling by the box. "Am I doing something wrong?" The owlet reached up and nibbled the mouse tail. He closed his eyes.

"Want the tail? Okay." He cut it off with his penknife and held it before Bardy. The owl took it in his beak and swallowed it.

"Good," he said. "Now eat the rest." Bardy took the mouse in his beak but did not swallow it.

"Eat," Leon said, and went back to bed.

In the morning he rose before the others and opened the owl box.

"Borden," he called. "Come here. The owl's dying."

It was Sally who arrived first.

"What owl?"

"Bardy," said her father, pointing.

"Oh, Pop," she exclaimed, dropping to her knees. "He's adorable." She pushed back her red, stringy curls. "What's wrong with him?"

"Won't eat."

"Who won't eat?" asked Cindy, Leon's wife, stepping into the kitchen. She had come home late last night and had not seen the owl box in the kitchen.

"An owlet," said Sally.

"Let me see it." Cindy got down on all fours and peered at the bird.

"Why, he's only a baby," she exclaimed. "He needs baby bites."

"Yeah," said Leon. "I guess that's what he was trying to tell me when he nibbled the tail—he wants little pieces."

"What kind of an owl is this?" Sally asked suspiciously.

"Barred owl," said Leon.

"Barred owl?" said Cindy. "Are you sure?"

"Of course I am," Leon replied. "I haven't been in the forests all my life not to know a barred owl when I see one."

"Are you really sure?"

"Of course he is," said Sally. "Pop knows owls, for goodness' sake."

Leon took one of the mice outside to the woodpile and chopped it into small pieces. He was going to tell the kids they would have to take care of the owlet if they wanted to keep it, but when he returned, Cindy was in the shower, Sally was washing pans, and Borden was still in bed. No one, he saw, was going to keep this owl alive but him. He knelt by the box and held out a morsel to Bardy. Bardy swallowed it with two thrusts of his head, closing his eyes as he did so.

"Hey, he's eating," Leon shouted. No one cheered, so he gave Bardy another bite, and another. Soon the mouse was gone and the second mouse, too.

"You ate two whole mice," he said to the owl.

Bardy's breast puffed out where the good food lay in his crop, the storage compartment in the throat of a bird. He fluttered his wings

and looked at Leon's face.

"More?" he asked. "You're crazy. That's all you get," and he went off to shower and dress.

When he returned, Borden and Sally were at the kitchen table eating breakfast cereal.

"Hey, Pop," Borden said, looking him over. "How come you got your 'Hickory' on? You shouldn't be in your work shirt today. It's Sunday."

"I'm going to the riverside field," he answered.

"Oh," said Borden, who had gotten home late and fallen into bed. He had not thought about the owlet until this moment. "How's Bardy?"

"I think he's dying," said Leon, picking up the sack of traps. "And I'm going to see to it that he lives until the court hearing—after which I'll wring his neck."

"Maybe you're not feeding him enough," said Sally. "Mr. James said barred owlets need big food—flying squirrels, gophers, rats—and lots of them."

"What were you talking to him for?" Leon snapped.

"I wasn't," said Sally. "I took his course. Remember?"

"He came by the station yesterday," said Borden. "He asked me to tell you he didn't mean to hit you—and that he had a summons too."

"Good." Leon smiled.

"I asked him how much food owlets need."

"Why did you do that?"

"You want the owl to live, don't you?" Borden snapped.

"What did he say?"

"Nine or ten mice a day."

"Nine or ten a day?" roared Leon. "He's not worth the effort."

"Better than paying a fine, isn't it?"

"Well, how do I know the judge will care?"

"Well, don't feed him, then," Sally said. She picked up the fuzzy bird and hugged him to her. "Wow, he's weak as jelly."

Bardy felt the warmth of Sally's body and snuggled against her. He rolled under his sharp claws so he would not injure her, just as his mother had done when she came into the nest.

Leon observed this without comment. Then he put on his slicker and went out into the pouring rain.

8

Two Night Owls

Leon caught only one mouse on Sunday. It was raining hard, and the mice were in their burrows chewing on roots. That night he waited until everyone had gone to bed. Then he set traps inside the house. He hoped a mouse or two might have come in out of the rain.

A sharp snap awoke him at 2 A.M. He slid out of bed and tiptoed to the kitchen. A young wood rat was in the trap under the sink.

He chopped it into delicate bites, lifted Bardy out of his box, and placed him on the kitchen table. The owlet sunk onto his heels and drooped his downy head.

"You don't look so good," Leon said.

"Come on, little fellow. You can't die on me. I'm depending on you. Got to make the nature lovers see cutters aren't all bad."

Leon lifted Bardy's head, opened his beak, and forced a morsel into his mouth. Bardy did not swallow. Leon stroked the slender throat, and the food slid down. For two hours, he force-fed the little owlet, and with each bite Bardy grew more alert.

"You're a good fellow," Leon said when the last bite was gone, and Bardy was perky enough to lift his head and focus on Leon's face. He fluttered his wings and begged for more food.

"I haven't got any more," Leon said helplessly. Then he looked at the refrigerator. "Chicken," he said. "Cindy bought a chicken today."

Leon cut up one chicken thigh, and when it was eaten, Bardy stopped begging. Leon rested his arms on the table and stared at the otherworldly creature, the elfin owl from the giant trees.

"You're shivering," he said, and glanced around nervously. Hearing no one awake, he picked up Bardy. "You stopped shaking when Sally cuddled you," he said, tucking the owlet in the crick of his arm. Bardy made soft noises and snuggled against the sleeve of Leon's terry-cloth bathrobe.

"Must be," he said almost gently, "that you still need your mother. I'll just take her place for a little while. No one can see us, and it might just keep you alive." He was embarrassed by this tender sentiment and added quickly, "—until the hearing, of course."

Leon took Bardy into the living room, turned the TV low, and sat down on the couch. The owlet pushed himself deeper into his warm arms and stopped shivering. He closed his eyes.

They were both asleep when the sun came up. Leon awoke with a start and hastily returned the owlet to his box. He did not want anyone to catch him hugging an owl, especially one whose neck he was going to wring

in a few days. And he was going to. By the misty light of dawn, he felt in charge of his destiny again. No owlet was going to run him.

The rain let up the next day, and Leon and Borden walked to the riverside field as the sun was coming up. Very quickly they trapped three mice and seven voles.

Leon had brought his fishing rod this morning. The half-pounders, young steelhead salmon that came up the rivers and streams this time of year, had been the great fish of Leon's boyhood. They swam through the water in silver streams, and he had caught them in silver streams, one right after another. But he had not seen any since he had been coming to the riverside field, and he wondered about them.

Borden picked up his pack to head off for school.

"Borden," Leon said, threading his line through the eyelets on the rod, "you have a minute? I'm worried about Bardy."

"What's wrong?"

"Those furry balls he spits out every day. You seen them?"

"Yeah. You can't miss them," Borden answered. "What's wrong with that?"

"Do you think he has some kind of disease?"

"Nah," Borden answered. "He hates fur, just like I hate liver. So we spit 'em out."

"Yeah, I'll bet that's it. Maybe I should peel the mice." Leon pulled out the line and fastened a lure to it.

"Aw, come on, Pop," Borden said. "Bardy knows what he's doing."

"I guess so." He was not convinced. "Find out about it, will you?"

"How?"

"You could ask Sally to ask that teacher."

Borden stared at his father. He was really hooked on Bardy.

He waved and trotted down the trail. If Bardy was ill, as his pop had suggested, they might have to take him to a vet. Borden resolved to find out about the fur balls.

That night Borden awoke Leon around

2 A.M. "Pop," he whispered, "I dreamed Bardy died. I don't dream stuff like that unless it's true. Come with me to check him, will you?"

Tiptoeing down the hall, Leon and Borden hesitated before Borden flicked on the kitchen light. Leon opened the owl box.

Bardy turned his black eyes upon him and stood up.

"Hi," Leon said, and grinned. "He looks alive to me."

"But not healthy," said Borden, glad that his nightmare was not true.

"He's shedding his baby feathers," said Leon, catching a wisp of down.

Leon lifted Bardy from his box, put him on the kitchen table, and sat down. His arm rested on the table. Bardy stumbled over to him and weakly climbed onto it. He stared devotedly at his rumpled mother.

"I'm still going to wring your neck," Leon said, and chuckled. "But right now you have to live." Bardy gazed at him as if he were waiting for something.

"What does he want?" Leon asked Borden.

"Maybe he's bored," Borden said. "He's a night owl, and there's nothing for him to do here at night, except watch TV."

"How about a little TV, Bardy?" Leon said, and got to his feet. Bardy walked up his arm to his shoulder. "That's what he wants," Leon said. "He wants a little action in his life." He gingerly stepped into the living room with Bardy on his shoulder. He stopped at the mirror.

"Hey, Borden," he said, looking at the reflection. "Bardy's a show, sitting on my shoulder. I'm going to take him to court with me. The judge will say, 'Aahhh, look at that cute little owl,' and tear up the fine."

"Pop, I'm going back to bed now," Borden said. "I'm tired."

"Go on," Leon answered. "I'll just sit here a minute. I'm not." He was smiling.

At 5:30 A.M. Leon was awakened by Bardy, who was gently rubbing his beak against his ear. Startled, Leon got to his feet.

"Thanks for waking me," he said. He listened to the house. No one was up. He went into the kitchen to put the owlet back in his box, but Bardy had other ideas. He dug his talons into Leon's bathrobe and would not let go.

"Come on," Leon whispered as he tried to take him off his shoulder. Bardy clung more tightly. Finally Leon lifted each talon and tucked it under the foot; then, holding Bardy's feet in his big hand, he lowered him into the box.

"You must be feeling better. You're talking to me again," he said.

"You're telling me you need a perch. You *are* getting older." He scratched his beard. "I guess it's time to get you out of the nest and into the forest."

The owlet gave Leon another penetrating look. This time Leon thought Bardy must be memorizing his face, he stared at him so deeply. He rubbed his scraggly beard. He was not a very pretty thing to memorize.

"But wait 'til the judge sees you look at me like that," he said. "He will put that teacher in jail and set me free." He chuckled, covered the box, and then briefly uncovered it.

"And by the way, Bardy," he said. "While you're sleeping today, I'm going to the coastal forest to cut a root sprout from a redwood stump. I'm going to make you a beautiful perch. From the way you gripped my arm, you're ready for one. Maybe Borden will help me." He smiled, glad for the privacy of darkness, then tiptoed off to bed.

9
Imprinting

Three days and twenty-nine mice later, Bardy had a perch. His body had fattened, and his head no longer drooped. When Leon put the perch down in the kitchen, Bardy hopped up onto it, shook his feathers, and sat up straight. Only the yellowish talons of his big feet showed beneath his pantaloons. White down still covered most of his body, but sable-brown feathers were beginning to appear on his back and wing coverts. He was becoming a juvenile owl, who would soon be adorned with the immature feathers of his species. They would be different from his baby down and different from the feathers he would wear as an adult next year.

Bardy turned around three times, shook, and tucked his head into his shoulder feathers. Soon he was asleep.

Leon and Borden had driven west to the redwood forests that grow along the coast to select this perch for Bardy. It was a burl, or sprout, that rises from the roots of the parent redwood and develops into a tree more swiftly than a seed.

Bardy's sprout was about two feet high with a rounded top, the perfect foothold for his big feet and curved talons. Leon had found it on the root of a stump in an area he had once helped to clear-cut. As he carried it to the truck, he stopped by the stream at the foot of the mountain. The water was opaque with mud. No salmon were spawning in the shallows. He looked up at the clear-cut mountainside.

"They were supposed to replant," he said to Borden. "Young trees would hold back this mud." He looked up at the devastation. "They never should have clear-cut."

"What should they have done?" Borden asked.

"Selected the big good ones. We had a good crew. We could have gotten them out without wiping out the forest. Been cheaper in the long run."

When Sally came home from school, she didn't go to her room and close the door anymore, but went right to the kitchen. She had taken it upon herself to change the newspapers under Bardy every day, vacuum his feathers, and put down fresh drinking water.

"I wish you'd keep your room as neat as you keep Bardy," Cindy said as Sally scrubbed Bardy's water dish.

"That's no fun," Sally answered. "Taking care of a cute little owlet is." She picked up a pellet and was about to throw it out when Borden came in from school to change to his work clothes.

"What's that all about?" he asked eagerly.

"It's a pellet," she said. "Owls eat their food whole. They cast what they can't digest

69

before they eat again. Why?"

"Pop wondered about them," Borden answered nonchalantly. "I'll tell him they're perfectly normal."

"They're so normal," Sally went on, "that if owls eat just beef and don't get the fur, bones, and feathers in rodents and birds, they won't be able to cast, and they'll get sickly. Birds of prey must cast."

Borden went into the living room to tell Leon about the pellets. He was watching his afternoon program with Bardy.

Cindy glanced through the door at the two couch potatoes.

"Goodness," she said. "I wish your father would find a job, any job. He worries about that bird all the time."

"He should read more about owls and stop worrying," Sally said. "I worry about what's going to happen to Bardy after the hearing."

"Borden's going to let him go," Cindy answered. "And Pop's going to kill him. Why?"

"Well," she said, "they may not be able to

do either." A curly smile moved from her lips to her eyes, and they twinkled. "Birds imprint on the people who raise and feed them."

"What does 'imprint' mean?" Cindy asked.

"It means they think the person nurturing them is 'Mother,' and that they look like that person. The love that 'mother' very much and follow her everywhere, even if it is a man or a robot. And that's not so good for Pop and Bardy."

"It's charming," said Cindy. "What's the matter with that?"

"It means," said Sally, "that Pop is Bardy's mom, and Bardy won't want to go back to the wild. And," she went on, "it also means Pop won't want to wring the neck of a little creature that loves him." Cindy put down the dish towel, turned around, and stared at Sally.

"Where have you learned all this?"

"From my science teacher, Mr. James."

"Sally." Cindy's eyes were wide, the pupils sharp. "Have you told that teacher about this owl?"

"No."

"Then why did he tell you about imprinting?"

"He told the Ecology Club about imprinting," Sally answered. "I belong to the Ecology Club."

"What?" Cindy gasped. "With Pop out of work because of ecology lovers, how could you join their club?"

"It's interesting," Sally answered.

"Your pop won't like it," Cindy said. "You'd better tell him right now."

"I'll tell him, but I'll tell him at the perfect time."

"What do you mean, the perfect time?"

"When Bardy is thoroughly imprinted on Pop, and Pop loves him." She considered her words and made them more accurate. "When they are bonded," she said.

Cindy shook her head, but she also smiled.

Leon came into the kitchen, put Bardy on his perch, said a few words, then went out the door.

The owlet crouched to follow Leon. He flapped his wings, but they were not strong enough to carry him in flight. He folded them to his body and pinned his eyes on the door through which Leon had gone. Sally watched the owlet with great interest.

"I think the perfect time is almost here," she said, sinking her fingers into the deep soft feathers on his head and scratching the little skull. "Don't you, pretty little owlet?" Bardy blinked slowly, bringing his lower lids toward the upper.

"You think he's your mom, don't you?" Sally said. "Do you think you look like him?"

"I think he does," said Cindy. "They both have beards and big black eyes."

10
Bonded

The next day Borden and Leon got up early as usual to go mousing before school. The day was warm, and Leon left the door open to blow out the birdy odors. Cindy had begun to complain about them. When they were in the alley behind their house, they heard a rasping hunger cry. Both turned to see Bardy following them on foot.

"Look who's coming," Borden said, and chuckled.

"Where do you think you're going, mister?" Leon said. Then, glancing right and left to make sure their neighbors weren't looking, he picked up the owlet and put him on his shoulder. "Okay, Bardy," he said. "You can

74

come. Maybe you'll catch yourself a mouse."

With Bardy posting on Leon's shoulder like a horseman, the three went down the trail to the abandoned field by the clear, rushing river.

As they approached, five crows came over the horizon. Cawing and screaming, they dove at Bardy. He jumped to his wings and tried to fly but only fluttered to the ground. Quickly Leon picked him up and tucked him inside his shirt. The crows flew above them, gaining height to strike again; but the enemy, the owl, had disappeared. They searched the field as they flew away.

Borden set the traps, and Leon sat down in the tall grass to hide Bardy from the crows. He took him out of his shirt and placed him on his knee. Bardy turned his head a full 145 degrees to the left and then to the right as he observed the trees and sky along the river. Then he lifted his feathers to say he was content. Leon sighed to say the same thing and tilted his face into the warm sun.

In that moment the grassland larks and sparrows saw Bardy and screamed their alarm cries. The crows heard and came racing back, blasting out frantically uttered caws that meant "Come harass the owl." Within seconds, twelve crows were diving and swooping at Bardy, cawing hysterically. Another was on its way to the fracas.

"Okay, okay," said Leon, and put Bardy back in his shirt.

"Guess we can't let Bardy out of the house again," Borden said. "The crows will tell the whole world we have an owl."

"Wonder what the owls did to the crows to get them so mad at them," Leon mused.

"Took their nests in the big trees, maybe," Borden said as he hoisted his school pack and headed toward town.

Several hours later, Leon put the owlet down in his backyard.

"I've got to know something, Bardy," he said, and took a few steps. Bardy took a few steps. Leon stopped. Bardy stopped. Leon ran

in a circle. Bardy ran in a circle. Leon hid behind the trash can, and, hopping and bouncing, Bardy found him.

"Scalawag," he said laughing. "You like me, don't you?" Picking him up, he carried him into the kitchen. "I'll take you to court, and you'll follow me right up to the judge."

He leaned down and almost kissed the round head. Then, horrified at himself, he blurted out, "And after that, I'll lead you up to the chopping block and chop off your head." Leon opened his mouth to laugh, but not even a chuckle came out.

A few days later when Sally was changing Bardy's papers, she took one of his tail feathers between her fingers.

"Pop," she said, frowning, "Bardy has hunger streaks." Leon put the morning's mouse catch in the refrigerator and came to look.

"What are hunger streaks?"

"See these tracks across each tail feather?" She pointed to a line in which there were no vanes. "Those are hunger streaks. He didn't get enough food when he was growing these feathers."

"What does it mean?" Leon asked. "He's not going to die, is he?"

"No," Sally said. "But he may have trouble flying. Feathers break at the hunger streaks, and he needs his tail to fly right."

"How do you know all this, Sally?" Leon asked.

"I learned it from Mr. James in the Ecology Club," she answered. "We're studying birds of prey."

The time was right to tell Leon about the club. Bardy loved Leon, and Leon loved Bardy. As Sally had surmised, Leon was not angry. However, he was a little miffed. He walked quickly away and turned on the TV. Above the din of the news, Sally heard him call, "Find out what you can about hunger streaks. It would be a terrible thing if Bardy couldn't fly."

11

The Shower Stall

After Borden left the riverside field for school, Leon and Bardy settled into their daily routine. Leon fished and Bardy slept from 9 A.M. to noon. They came home and ate their respective lunches of canned soup and mice. They then watched TV. Around 2 P.M. they drove along the Trinity River. Leon would park, get out, and cast his line from time to time as he looked for the half-pounders of his youth. Bardy followed him along the riverbank, jumping on moving leaves and snagging bobbing flowers in his talons. Leon caught no steelheads. He looked up at the treeless mountainsides.

At 5 P.M. Bardy and Leon returned to the house. Leon made supper for the family, and

Bardy owl-dozed, eyes almost shut, breast feathers touching his beak. His vibrissae stood up like sea urchin spines.

After dinner was Borden's time to play with Bardy. He wanted to teach him to fly. It was his dream to see him take off for the mountains. He would hold out a tantalizing bite of mouse and not let Bardy eat it until he flew to his hand for it. At first Bardy hopped a foot along the top of the couch, then two feet; but when Borden got four feet away, he would turn his back and watch TV.

On school nights everyone was in bed by 10 P.M. and Bardy in his box. At 1 A.M. the alarm clock went off, and Leon got up. He would put Bardy on the back of the living room couch and turn on the TV. Eyes wide open, head swinging, the owlet concentrated on the action on the screen like his parents concentrated on flying squirrels. He liked Westerns, with their horses that galloped across the landscape. If he could have flown, he would have nailed one.

The hearing was scheduled for the third Tuesday in June. Borden was in the kitchen when Leon received the papers from the judge. He was surprised that his father did not give his usual tirade against the law and spotted owls, but he didn't. Borden was glad.

Leon tucked the papers into the kitchen drawer and went off to shower. Borden made himself a sandwich and picked up *Car and Driver*.

While he was reading, Bardy spread his wings, fluttered downward, and landed softly at Borden's feet. Wings over his back, he ran across the kitchen floor and down the hallway. The bathroom door was slightly ajar, and Bardy went in.

The shower stopped, then went on again. Next the bathroom door flew open. "Borden!" Leon boomed. "Come here."

Borden put down his magazine, skidded around the corner, and bolted down the hall, expecting to find a water main broken or a the house on fire. He saw nothing.

"He's taking a shower with me!" Leon exclaimed, running out of the bathroom with a towel around his waist.

"Who's taking a shower with you?"

"Bardy." Leon pulled back the curtain. There in the stall stood the little owlet. He flipped his wings, stood under the spray, and splashed his breast feathers in the water. He repeated the ceremony again and again.

"He loves it," said Borden. Bardy looked up, saw that Leon was not with him, and fluttered to the edge of the shower stall. He tried to climb out, but could not. He was too heavy with water. Giving up, he let go and washed toward the drain.

"He's drowning," Leon cried.

"Turn off the shower," said Borden, and did it himself. The water stopped. Bardy looked up. His feathers were plastered against his body, and he was half his normal size.

"He's going to die," said Leon.

"So?" Borden said. "You're just going to wring his neck."

"I want him to live," Leon said passionately, then added calmly, "long enough for me to make a good impression on the judge."

The big rugged cutter carefully wrapped the small wet owl in a towel and handed him to Borden.

"Take him to the kitchen," he said. "Turn on the oven. Put him on the open door and let him dry off while I get dressed. He's shivering."

Borden stared at his father. He really did care about the owlet.

Borden did as Leon asked. He turned on the oven and put Bardy on the open door. Then he went back to his magazine. In a few minutes Bardy felt the heat and ran into the warm cave. He shook, preened, and fluffed his feathers.

The metal grew hotter and hotter, and by the time Leon arrived, Bardy was picking up one foot, and then the other. He shifted his feet faster and faster, then abruptly ran out of the oven. He jumped on his wings and plunged toward the floor. Leon reached out and caught him.

"Borden," he snapped. "What's the matter with you? You let him burn his feet." He put Bardy on his back in his left hand and gently took first one big foot, then the other in his fingers.

"He's okay," he said, with a trace of relief in his voice. "He got himself out of there in time with no thanks to you. Get Sally's hair dryer. I've got to get this little fellow warm."

Borden knocked on Sally's door. Her boom box was turned on high, so he opened the door and stuck his head in.

"Can I come in?" he asked. "Pop wants to borrow your hair dryer."

"Pop wants to borrow my hair dryer? What on earth for?"

"Bardy took a shower with him, and he wants to give him a blow-dry." He grinned.

Sally picked up her dryer and ran out the door with Borden at her heels.

"Pop," she said excitedly. "Guess what I learned today?"

"What?"

"That the last thing little birds do before they fly is bathe. Bardy bathed. That means he's going to fly today or tomorrow."

"Fly?" Leon said.

"Fly," Sally repeated. "Out over town and back to the mountain."

"He can't do that until the hearing," Leon stated firmly.

"Well, then, you'll have to jess him," she said, turning on the dryer and letting the warm air fall gently on Bardy.

"Jess him?"

"Put leather straps on his leg—falconry style. They're called jesses. You put a leash on the jesses and tether the leash to his perch. He can't fly away."

"I suppose you know someone who could do that?"

"Yes."

"Well, I'm not interested." But his tone was not convincing.

12

Flying Lessons

Upon learning that Bardy was soon to fly, Leon changed his mind about having him walk behind him down the aisle of the courthouse. Now he envisioned him flying grandly over the heads of lawyers and court clerks. Borden would let Bardy sit on his fist. Leon would walk up to the judge and call the owl. Bardy would fly across the courtroom, alight on Leon's fist, and nibble his ear lovingly. The judge would marvel, grow mellow, and say, "Case dismissed."

Leon no longer said what he would do to Bardy after that.

One morning on the river shore when Borden had departed for school, he put Bardy on a tree stump and stood in front of him.

"Okay," he said. "Borden's not doing so well with you, so I'm going to give you flying lessons. Do what I do." He flapped his arms. Bardy flapped his wings. Leon ran in a big circle, flapping. Bardy took off from the stump, sailed to the ground, and ran in a big circle, flapping. As he ran and flapped, the flapping lifted him off the ground. Quick to correct his error, he came down. He ran behind his mother.

Leon halted.

"So much for that," he said. "You make a very good human being, but you're a lousy owl. You've got to fly, Bardy, fly. Fly over people's heads, around the court, and down to my hand." He put the owlet back on the stump. "Are you always going to walk like me?" he asked. "Don't you know you're supposed to fly?" The owlet looked up at a passing swallow.

"That's it," Leon said enthusiastically. "Do what he does. Fly like a swallow." But Bardy felt no connection between the soaring bird and himself. When Leon walked off to check the traps, Bardy hopped to the ground and walked behind him.

They went home early. Leon had been asked to join a group of cutters, truck drivers,

and hook tenders, the men who wrestled the trees from the forest. Almost all had suffered broken knees or legs, torn muscles, and blows from falling or rolling wood, yet they loved their work and had asked a national TV network to let them tell their side of the controversy. They were to meet in the park at noon.

Leon gave Bardy a mouse. Bardy swallowed it whole.

"Hey, you've grown up," Leon said. "Looks like I don't have to cut up your food anymore. Good boy." Bardy hopped to the couch. With beak and feet, he climbed to his perch and settled down to watch TV. Leon turned on the set and sat.

"You know, Bardy," he said. Bardy hopped to his shoulder. "I'm not going to that meeting. Even if they lift the ban, it won't help us lumbermen for long. When all the big trees are cut down, we won't have jobs anyway."

Every day Bardy joined Leon in the shower. It was one of his great pleasures. He preened, and splashed water up under his wings and into his head feathers. When he discovered that the other members of his family also took showers, he joined them, too.

One day Borden forgot to lift him out of the stall, and the owlet sat there wet and bedraggled for almost an hour before Leon found him. Leon dried him off, then took out a sheet of paper and a marker. He made a sign that said: **REMOVE OWL AFTER SHOWERING**. He hung it by the shower stall.

At 1 A.M., the alarm went off, and Leon took Bardy into the living room for his early-morning Western. "You know, Bardy," he said as the owlet hopped to the back of the couch, "it's a good thing you're not a spotty. I've come to like you a lot."

About a week later, Jimmy Olden came by the gas station and asked Borden if he could work some of Borden's hours.

"I really need the money," he said. "My pop's out of work."

"Your pop?" exclaimed Borden. "But he's a fisherman. The river's full of fish."

"No, it isn't," Jimmy replied. "Not many salmon are coming up the Trinity anymore."

"They aren't?" said Borden. "How come?"

"Overfishing with gill nets in the ocean, my dad said, and clear-cutting inland. Clear-cutting erodes the soil, mud gets in the streams and creeks, and fish eggs suffocate. No fish."

Borden stood quietly, thinking about what Jimmy had said. Then he picked up his coat. "You can work right now, if you want. I have some things I ought to do."

13

Broken Feathers

Borden biked out to the riverside to find Pop and Bardy. Leon had taken the truck today, and it was parked some distance from the river. He was not in sight, but Bardy was. He was sitting upright on the steering wheel of the pickup, half asleep, half awake.

"Come on," Borden said to the owlet, "I'll give you a ride out to Pop."

Borden stuck out his arm, and Bardy walked to his shoulder. Borden pushed down on the pedals and wheeled off. He had not gone far before the owlet hopped onto the handlebars. He opened his wings and bent his body into the wind. The feathers on his lids lowered to protect his eyes.

"Hey," Borden said. "You like this, don't you." He laughed and swung back to the road. He circled around and around, and the faster he went, the more serene the owlet became. He seemed, Borden thought, to be soaring over his great forest of ancient trees, looking for the arbutus garden where Borden had found him.

"I'm going to take you to your home as soon as you can fly, little Bardy," he promised. "You must miss the big trees."

Leon came down the riverbank with a small fish for Bardy. It wiggled wildly. Bardy leaped onto his wings and flapped them. He never reached the fish. He was flying. He pulled down and up and climbed higher. Above the blue-green water of the Trinity, he cricked one wing, turned, and soared back.

"He can fly!" shouted Borden.

"He can fly!" Leon cried out.

As he drifted silently toward them, a gust of wind came up the valley and struck him. He lost control and plummeted downward, flapping backward to break his descent. He crash-landed on the grass. Leon reached him first.

"Borden," he called. "Come here. Bardy has broken his tail." Borden put down his bike and ran to Leon. All but two of Bardy's tail feathers had broken off about an inch below his body.

"They broke along the lines of the hunger streaks," said Borden, "just like Sally said they would. Now what do we do?"

"Maybe he can fly without a tail," said Leon. "You hold him on your fist. I'll call to him like I'll do in court."

Borden held Bardy high. Leon gave a hoot. Bardy lowered his body and spread his wings. He jumped into the air, flapped his wings, and crashed to the ground.

"He can't steer without his tail," said Borden.

"Well, we don't need jesses," Leon said. "He's not going anywhere." Leon leaned down, and Bardy stepped up onto his hand. "And I'm glad of that. Sally was going to ask *that man* how to make them."

"This is terrible, Pop," said Borden. "How can I let him go if he can't fly?"

"Who said you're going to let him go?"

"I did, Pop. I found him. I want to take him back to the big trees." He looked at Leon. "That's the only thing we can do, because you aren't going to wring his neck. You just couldn't."

"We'll see about that," said Leon, letting Bardy climb to his shoulder. He took him back to the truck. "Couldn't wring his neck. Humph," said Leon.

Borden watched Leon drive off. When he was out of sight, he picked up his bike and headed for the high school.

It was Tuesday afternoon, and the Ecology Club was meeting. He sat on the steps outside the laboratory door and waited for Sally. He did not go into the classroom. He certainly would not be caught dead in that room with that man. Let Sally betray Pop, but not him.

When Sally appeared, Borden called to her.

"What are you doing here?" she asked in surprise.

"I need to talk to you."

"What about?"

"Bardy's feathers broke off at the hunger streak line. He can't fly."

"New feathers will grow in."

"When?"

"Next year."

"Next year?" he said, as Paul James came through the door with several students. "We can't wait that long. After the hearing, Pop's going to wring his neck." He glanced at the teacher and back at Sally. "Didn't you tell me that falconers know how to mend broken feathers?"

"If they do," Sally said, "Mr. James would know. He's a falconer. Ask him."

Borden hesitated and thought of Pop.

"You know him," he said. "You ask him." He backed away, picked up his bike, and walked it down the pavement, glancing back at Sally now and then. She was talking to the teacher, and from the look on his face, Borden knew she was asking the right questions.

He took the trail through the town's tourist attraction, a park of huge, ancient trees. He stopped on the bridge over the stream. The water was crystal clear. Among the rocks, green and pink lights played off the scales of darting fish. He looked at the uncut forest and thought about Jimmy's pop.

Sally was late coming home. Borden heard her footsteps on the walk and hurried to meet her.

"What did he say?" he asked, following her into the kitchen. Leon and Bardy were in the shower.

"He said when falcons break feathers, the falconers 'imp,' or graft, feathers on them. That means they push good feathers into the quills of the broken ones and fasten them there with glue and thread." From her school backpack, she took out twelve brick-red feathers. "Tail feathers," she said.

"Where did you get them?"

"*That man*," she said sarcastically, "found a red-tailed hawk that had been shot. He had it in the lab freezer and gave me the tail feathers. They are about the same size as a barred owl's. We'll imp them on. *He* told me how."

"Who are you talking about?" Leon asked,

as he walked into the kitchen with Bardy on one hand and Sally's hair dryer in the other.

"A falconer," said Borden. "He told Sally how to fix broken feathers on a bird."

"Will it hurt him?"

"No," said Sally. "Birds have no feeling in their feathers, like our hair and fingernails."

"Well," said Leon. "Let's do it."

"I thought you were going to wring his neck," Sally could not help saying.

"Who said I was going to wring his neck?" Leon snapped. Then he harumphed and plugged in the dryer.

14
Borden Sees Spots

Sally struggled as she measured and cut the red-tailed hawk feathers to the right length and the shafts to the right shape. Carefully she picked up Bardy. When she turned him over on his back to work on his tail, he snapped his beak and struck out with his strong, sharp talons.

"How am I going to do this?" she said. "He doesn't like it."

"I'll hold him," said Leon. "I know a trick." He gently picked up the owlet and placed him breast up in one big hand. With the other he stroked his breast until the owlet slipped into a trance and lay still.

"Where did you learn that?"

"When we raised chickens. We'd put them in a trance before we wrung their necks." Borden did not look up. Sally winced.

An hour later Sally had four of the eleven feathers imped, but they were too loose. She looked at her father in desperation.

"This is all just too silly," she blurted. "We're talking around Mr. James. When are we going to admit that he is the source of all our knowledge about this owlet, and ask him to come over here? We need him."

"Not in my house," said Leon.

Borden suddenly stood motionless, staring at Bardy. His mouth dropped open, his eyes widened.

The owlet's new breast feathers had white spots on them. He knew the truth. He knew it all too well. He had seen that spotted owl hanging from the lamppost in the park very clearly.

"I think I'll let him go tomorrow, anyway," Borden said. His voice was squeaky from his effort to be nonchalant.

"No, sir," said Leon "I'm going to take him

to the hearing. I want the judge to see what a gentle guy I am."

Sally heard the alarm in her brother's voice. She looked at him. He was still staring at Bardy. She looked at the owlet, then at Borden and back to the owlet. She looked long. And then she, too, saw the very pale spots and was horrified.

"Yeah, Pop," she said. "We'll let him go tomorrow." Borden looked at her. She looked at him, and the exchanged glances each said to the other, "Bardy's a spotted owl."

"Borden," Leon said, stroking Bardy to keep him still, "there's some epoxy in the drawer by the sink. Let's try that." Mouth hanging open, Borden obeyed. Sally tried to stick a hawk feather dipped in epoxy into the owl's feather stub. The pungent odor awoke Bardy, and he flopped over in Leon's hand. The feather fell out.

"All right, all right," Leon roared. "Call the goon. I want Bardy to fly when I hoot to him in front of the judge."

"No," said Borden. "We don't need to call Mr. James."

"No, we don't," said Sally stiffly. "I can fix the feathers. Hold him still again."

"What's going on?" Cindy asked. She had just come home from work to find her family huddled in the kitchen.

"We're imping," Borden said. "Bardy broke his tail feathers."

"You'd think you two owl haters liked that bird," she said. "When are you crazies going to let him go?"

"Tomorrow," said Borden.

"As soon as I fix his tail," said Sally. Cindy looked over her shoulder.

"After the hearing I'll wring his neck," said Leon, but nobody paid any attention to him.

"I can do that," she said. "Let me have him."

"You know how to imp?" Sally asked in amazement.

"You kids always seem surprised that I

know anything at all," she said, rolling up her sleeves. "I didn't breed parrots when I was a kid without learning something about feathers and imping.

"Now get me a safety razor blade, a needle, and some dental floss."

Cindy's fingers moved swiftly and assuredly, and before dark, Bardy had a gorgeous red-tailed hawk's tail.

"Look at that," said Borden. "No one would ever know what kind of an owl he is

now. Whoever heard of an owl with a red tail with a black border on it?" He chuckled.

"Thanks, Mom," said Sally. "I'll fix dinner. You take a rest."

"Well, I don't mind if I do," Cindy said.

"I'll peel the potatoes," said Borden.

"I'll set the table," said Leon.

Cindy held out a morsel of food to Bardy. He flew across the kitchen on his new tail and perched on her hand.

"He can fly," she said triumphantly, and carried him into the living room, where she put him on the back of the couch, turned on the TV, and picked up the newspaper.

"Listen to this," she called. " 'The President Will Hear Both Sides of Owls, Jobs, and Old Trees Controversy.' " She read on in silence, then aloud. " 'The Vice President will head up a study group. Both will be in Portland, Oregon, at the end of the month.' "

"Wow," said Sally. "That's great."

"We lumbermen will be trampled," Leon said, and poked Sally's hamburgers to see if they were done.

"Let's eat," called Borden.

Cindy folded the newspaper, and as she did, closed it over an insert she had not read:

> **FOR AN INDIVIDUAL**
>
> **OR CORPORATION**
>
> **KILLING OR POSSESSING**
>
> **A THREATENED OR ENDANGERED SPECIES,**
>
> **THE PENALTY IS**
>
> **A $200,000 FINE**
>
> **AND UP TO ONE YEAR IN PRISON.**

15
Paul James

The Vice President of the United States was coming to Fresta. Borden heard the news at the gas station and called Pop.

"He wants to talk to the lumbermen and the environmentalists," he said. "He hopes we can have trees, owls, *and* cutters. He's crazy, isn't he?"

"Oh, I don't know," said Leon. Borden looked at the telephone to make certain it was working correctly.

"When's he coming?" Leon asked.

"Monday," Borden answered.

"Good," Leon said. "I'll bring Bardy. The Veep will see that cutters care about owls—except the kind that takes our jobs."

"I wouldn't do that if I were you, Pop." Borden's voice was sharp with urgency.

"Why not? He's cute. The Veep will like him. Points for the lumbermen."

Borden was about to tell Leon that Bardy was a spotted owl, but thought better of it. He just might wring his neck or chop off his head. Even though Leon loved Bardy the barred owl, he could never love Bardy the spotted owl.

"Speak up, Borden. Why shouldn't I take Bardy to meet the Veep?"

"We put a red tail on him."

"Looks good."

"Maybe owl lovers won't like it."

"So much the better."

That wasn't going to scare Pop. He thought again.

"The conservation officer won't let you keep him," Borden said in desperation. "Sally said birds of prey are protected by law. He'll be confiscated."

"What kind of nonsense is that?" said Pop. "He'd be dead if we hadn't saved him."

"Pop," said Borden. "I'm coming home at four. I really want to let Bardy go. I want to take him back where I found him."

"No, siree," said Leon, and hung up.

As Borden biked homeward at full speed, he came upon Sally walking home through the town park.

"Want a ride, Sal?" he called.

"You bet," she said. "You and I need to talk."

"We sure do. I mean we really do! We've got to figure out how to save Bardy—and Pop! He loves that owl, you know."

"I do know. And think what his friends will do when they find out he has a spotted owl."

Borden's eyes widened. "Oh, wow," he said.

"Let's go to the Pizza Palace," Sally suggested. "Maybe we can figure out what to do before we go home."

Sally wiggled onto the handlebars, and Borden wheeled past the gazebo now trimmed with red, white, and blue garlands. Posters were being hung from trees and lampposts: PEOPLE NOT OWLS; SUPPORT YOUR LOCAL SPOTTED OWL—FROM A ROPE; OLD GROWTH CANNOT BE REPLACED. The bandmaster and the town electrician were setting up equipment for the band and the speakers. Police barriers were stacked by the gazebo. Strangers were everywhere.

"Secret Service," whispered Sally. "This is big stuff."

Off to themselves in a corner of the Pizza Palace, Borden suggested that he take Bardy to the mountain while Sally lured Pop into the garage to paint protest posters.

"No," Sally said. "That's deceitful. Let's ask Judge Kramer to hold the hearing tomorrow. When that's over, Pop might let him go."

"I doubt it," Borden said. "I doubt both things. Judge Kramer changing the date, and Pop letting Bardy go when it's over." They sipped diet sodas, nodded to their classmates, and worried.

The door opened, and Paul James came

in. He saw Sally and Borden, smiled, and walked over to their table. Ordinarily Borden wouldn't have tolerated sitting at the same table with the science teacher, but now he was desperate.

"Won't you sit down, Mr. James?" Borden asked.

"How's the owl?" he said as he pulled up his chair.

"He looks very fancy in his new red tail," Sally answered.

"Can he fly?"

"Yes," she said. "The imped feathers work. He can fly across the living room to the couch."

"Bardy won the battle of the big trees in our house," Borden said. "Pop the owl hater is now Pop the owl lover."

"But does he also love spotted owls?" Paul James asked. Sally had told him they had a barred owl.

"Well," said Borden, wishing he had never spoken, "he probably doesn't."

"You should tell him the barred owl is part of the old-growth forest, too," Paul James said. "It's not just spotted owls that we want to save, but barred owls, flying squirrels, butterflies, martens, deer, ancient trees, clear water, and salmon."

"And the silence," said Borden. "It's pretty nice in the old growth."

"Yes, it is. I have to admit that the silence is the greatest value of the old growth, to me.

But it has other values to other people—lumber, hunting, recreation, fishing. Whatever it is, the giant trees are running out. Your pop may have to train for a new job," Paul James said.

"That's what Jimmy's pop is doing," Borden said. "He can't fish anymore. No salmon. He's taking a course in making recreational boats. There are lots of pretty rivers and lakes in this country."

Paul James nodded his approval and rose.

"I've got to be going," he said. "I want to get my research papers ready to give to the Vice President's committee." He looked down at the two young kids with great understanding. The people of Fresta were suffering for something that never should have happened—the ravaging of the old-growth forests. These kids were the victims. "I'm glad your owl can fly" was all he could think to say.

"By the way, Mr. James," Sally said, as the teacher turned to leave. "When is your hearing?"

"I don't have one," he answered. "I paid the fine. The fight was ridiculous, and I'm sorry for it." He patted Sally's shoulder and left the restaurant.

"Now what do we do?" said Borden, getting up from the table.

"Go home," said Sally, "and tell Pop he has a spotted owl and that we have to let him go."

16

The Old Growth

Leon opened the front door as Borden and Sally pulled up to the house and Sally got off the bike.

"Where have you been?" he shouted.

"At the Pizza Palace," Borden said. "What's the matter?"

"Where did you find Bardy, Borden?"

"Up the mountain above Fire Creek."

"Take me there."

"Now?"

"Now. We have to let Bardy go."

Sally stared at her father. Borden straddled the bar and gaped at him.

"Everything all right?" asked Sally meekly.

"No," Leon said, holding out the newspaper. "Read this." His thick forefinger tapped the printed insert Cindy had folded away without reading.

"Two-hundred-thousand-dollar fine for killing or possessing a threatened or endangered species," Leon said.

"Wow," said Borden, and looked at Sally. He whispered, "Are barred owls a threatened species?"

"No."

"Then he knows what Bardy is," Borden said under his breath. "Let's go."

"You two get in the truck." Leon turned toward the hallway. "I'll be right out with Bardy. I want to stop by the post office on our way and mail a letter."

The owlet rode out of the house on Leon's broad shoulder, fanning his red tail as if he knew it was special. Sally and Borden looked at their rugged pop, walking down the steps with the red-tailed owlet.

"What a strange pair," Sally whispered, mostly to herself.

"Crazy, if you think about it," said Borden. "Pop saved the life of his worst enemy. If this was a spy movie, they'd call Bardy 'The Insider.' He came right into our midst and turned us all around. I'll never be able to look at an owl the same way again."

"Well, this story's not over yet," Sally said, and Leon climbed into the driver's seat and

pulled out of the driveway. Bardy hopped to Borden's shoulder and stuck his head out of the window.

Leon stopped at the post office, then drove past Mike's Gas Station to the mountain road. A mile out of town he turned onto a dirt logging road and drove through miles of clear-cut forest to the ridge.

"Park there," Borden said, pointing to a turnaround under a Douglas fir.

"Hey, I know this place," said Leon, slowing down and coming to a stop. "I cut around here. Used to be a spotted owl's nest on the side of that steep ravine."

"Bardy's nest," Borden said. "You showed it to me."

Enrique looked down from his Douglas fir as three people got out of the truck cab and walked across the road. He bobbed his head and swirled it from left to right, the better to see with his ears. He heard the flowers of the bleeding heart dance on their stems as the people brushed them, and the warning click of a varied thrush when they walked too close to his nest. The moist forest absorbed all other sounds.

Leon, Bardy, Sally, and Borden stopped on the edge of the ravine and looked into the stately forest. Each massive tree was backlit with an umbra of silver needles. They stood quietly.

"Pop," Sally finally said, "when did you know Bardy was a spotted owl?"

"I'm not sure," he answered. "I guess I knew all along, but didn't want to admit it. I like Bardy."

Borden walked to the arbutus garden.

"Here's where I found him," he said. "But his nest is halfway down the ravine, if you think we should put him there."

"We'll put him back where you found him," Leon said, and picked up a sturdy branch. He pushed it into the soft soil.

"Sit here, Bardy," he said. "Your parents will come and get you."

"What if they don't?" Sally asked.

"Then we'll have to feed him every day until he can hunt. He can't catch his own food yet," Leon continued thoughtfully, "and I've noticed he won't do anything until he's good and ready—like kids."

Leon lifted Bardy from his shoulder and showed him the perch. He flew to it, hunched down, and stared up and around at the forest.

From his pocket Leon took two mice. He placed them beside Bardy on the perch.

"Do you think he'll recognize his parents?" Sally asked. "After all, he's imprinted on you. He thinks you're his mom."

"He'll know them," Leon said. "There's something about kin. Even pollywogs know their brothers and sisters. Some guy color-marked several hatches of pollywogs, then mixed them all up and put them in a big tank.

"The blue family got together with the blues, the reds got together with the reds, and the greens ganged up with the greens. Bardy will do just fine. He's a whole lot smarter than a pollywog."

"Where did you learn about pollywogs?" Sally asked in amazement.

"From your ecology book," he said.

Sally and Borden looked at each other. Pop was changing their idea of him with every minute that passed. They silently rearranged their thoughts. Leon filled the soundless gap.

" 'Know your enemy,' I said to myself. So I read Paul James's lectures you left on the kitchen table, and some of the pamphlets he gave you, Sally." He turned away. "Come on. Let's go home."

Sally took one last look at Bardy and followed Leon. Borden hung back, stroking Bardy's head and talking to him. Borden picked a piece of dust from his back and examined the new tail.

"I found him on the ground Pop," Borden called. "Wouldn't he be better there?"

"No," said Leon. "He's just fine where he is."

"When he's this old, he should be up in the bushes," Sally said. "In a few months he will perch higher. Next he'll fly and learn to hunt." Still Borden would not turn away. He put his fingers under Bardy's beak and lifted his head until the huge black eyes looked into his own. "I love you, owlet," he whispered. "Good luck."

17
The Nobleman

Leon led them away through the forest. "Want to see a nobleman?" he called.

"I guess so," Borden answered.

"I'd like to see it, " Sally said, eager to do something before she cried.

"What is it?" asked Borden.

"A Douglas fir," Leon answered.

"Oh," said Sally, surprised to hear the affectionate note in his voice. "You're going to show us a big tree?"

Leon put his arms around their shoulders and led the two spotted owlet lovers along the ridge, then down a steep ravine.

He took them down the slope past Bardy's nest tree and dense rhododendron groves. He took them through purple-blue shadows and under mammoth trees where sword fern communities grew eight feet tall. Near the bottom of the ravine he pushed back a big-leaf maple branch and, as if he had opened a door, showed his children a kingdom of ancient trees. One was as large as a prairie silo. An emerald variety of wild mosses and ferns grew over its roots and trunk.

"Oh," said Sally softly. "It's not a nobleman, it's a king."

"It has orange spray on it," said Borden. "Doesn't that mean it's going to be cut?"

"My boss marked it several years ago. He told me to cut it."

"But you didn't?" said Borden.

"Did the judge's order save it?" Sally asked.

"No," Leon said, patting the tree. "We clear-cut over there." He pointed to the empty mountainside. "But when I saw this tree, I told my boss I couldn't cut it."

"You couldn't?" Sally and Borden said simultaneously, delight and pride in their voices.

"No," said Leon. "Look at it. I couldn't lay it down without knocking down those three big incense cedars and that prime western hemlock. I wouldn't do that—that's not my style."

"Oh," Borden said.

Leon looked up through the gracefully whorled branches to the flattened needles with their bright-green undersides. "A real nobleman," he said. "Stumped me, all right. Great tree." He slapped its mossy trunk and laughed.

"You like old trees?" Borden was now quite perplexed.

"I love old trees," Leon said. "They challenge me. This old fellow has been working eight hundred years to get the better of me. Look what it did. Grew up on steep hillside I can barely climb. Then it let a grove of cedars surround it, and bushes and windfall. I walked around it forty times but couldn't figure out how to drop it without killing myself and wiping out the grove. Quite a dilemma. But it did do something nice for me." He walked into a space between two huge buttresses. "Here's where I ate my lunch out of the rain." Sally and Borden crept into the shelter with him and looked out at the shafts of silver sunlight spearing down through the mist. A junco sang, a winter wren caroled, and a brown creeper chattered as it ran up, then down the great king.

"Let's bring the Veep here," Borden said. "He'd like to see this tree, I'll bet."

"Well, if we did, I'd tell him this," Leon said. "I can cut it for you. I'll take out that nice straight seventy-five-year-old Douglas fir over there." He pointed. "And I'll take out the giant western hemlock right here. I can drop both of them without hitting any other tree. The two would bring a nice profit and let in the sun. I'd plant Douglas firs in that sun. They need lots of sunshine when they're young. Then I'd stop cutting for twenty-five years.

"I'd leave the nobleman for campers and

picnickers. This is a pretty place."

"Pop, I didn't know you knew forestry," Sally said.

Leon smiled. "You can't be a cutter all your life and not know something about the way forests work. Come on, I'll show you something else.

"This is the way a stream should be," Leon said. "Not like that muddy rut at the bottom of the clear-cut mountain where we got Bardy's perch."

"Did clear-cutting really do that?"

"Sure did."

"Gosh, Pop," Borden said. "Your work put Jimmy Olden's pop out of work. He's a fisherman, and there are no more salmon coming up the streams around here anymore."

"Yeah," Leon said. "It's like a game of dominoes. Who will fall next?"

"The canneries," said Borden. "Then the tin-can makers, then the truckers, then the merchants, then the banks, then the—"

"—people who eat fish," said Leon. "Then

the babies who need vitamin D from fish—
So let's get back to the trees and start over."

Borden waded into the icy stream and turned over a rock. He caught a crayfish, looked at it, and put it back. Sally found a frog.

They climbed back to the arbutus garden in the summer twilight.

Bardy was gone.

"Oh," cried Sally. "I miss him."

Leon and Borden looked at the empty perch and hurried to the logging road. At the truck, Leon leaned down and picked up an owl's pellet. He looked up.

"Hi, Bardy," he said. Sally ran across the road.

"There are two of them," she said. She was pointing to a shadowy owl shape a few feet above Bardy.

"But it's not a spotted owl," said Leon. "It's red."

"Yeah, it is," Borden said with great disappointment. He wanted Bardy to be with his family.

"Let's go," Leon said, but no one moved. All three stood quietly, watching their wonderful friend.

A puff of red dust appeared above Bardy. Then a second and a third cloud arose, and where the red owl had been sat Enrique. His spots shone like stars in the twilight.

"Well, I'll be danged," Leon said. "It's Bardy's pop, Enrique, the cutters' owl."

"Hey, Bardy," Borden called. "You'd better bring your dusty old pop to the house for a shower."

"But there won't be any mice," Leon called to him. "I've got a job. Starts Tuesday. The fish hatchery needs a good man this season." Borden and Sally stared at him. "When that's done, who knows? Maybe I'll even see if I can get a job showing those environmentalists where to find the last fish in the last clean streams up here, and"—he glanced at Bardy—"spotted owls. If they're going to save them, they'd better know where they are." He grinned. "I can tell those environmentalists a lot about these forests and save them a lot of legwork."

"What about the judge?" Borden asked. "How can you go to work on Tuesday? That's the day of the hearing."

"Oh, that," said Leon. "I mailed him a money order on the way up here. Paid the fine. I've got better things to do than argue with a judge."

Bardy heard Pop's voice and flew to a low branch. He fluttered his wings and called for food. Leon looked up, swallowed the lump that was rising in his throat, and quickly opened the truck door. Bardy crouched to fly to him, but Leon disappeared inside the truck. As they drove away, Borden watched Bardy for as long as he could through the rear window.

When he could no longer hear the noise of the truck, Enrique dropped to his side, a flying squirrel in his beak. Bardy sidled over to him. He stared intently at his father's face. It matched that face of long ago, when he was fed by his father instead of his mother. He had been very young then, and the round disc and those two caring eyes were permanently imprinted on his memory. He fluttered his wings, and his father fed him. Bardy was home.

———

Night came to the old-growth forest. Bardy dozed. Enrique flew to the Douglas fir and called to his mate. He called again, then over and over and over—but no owl answered him.